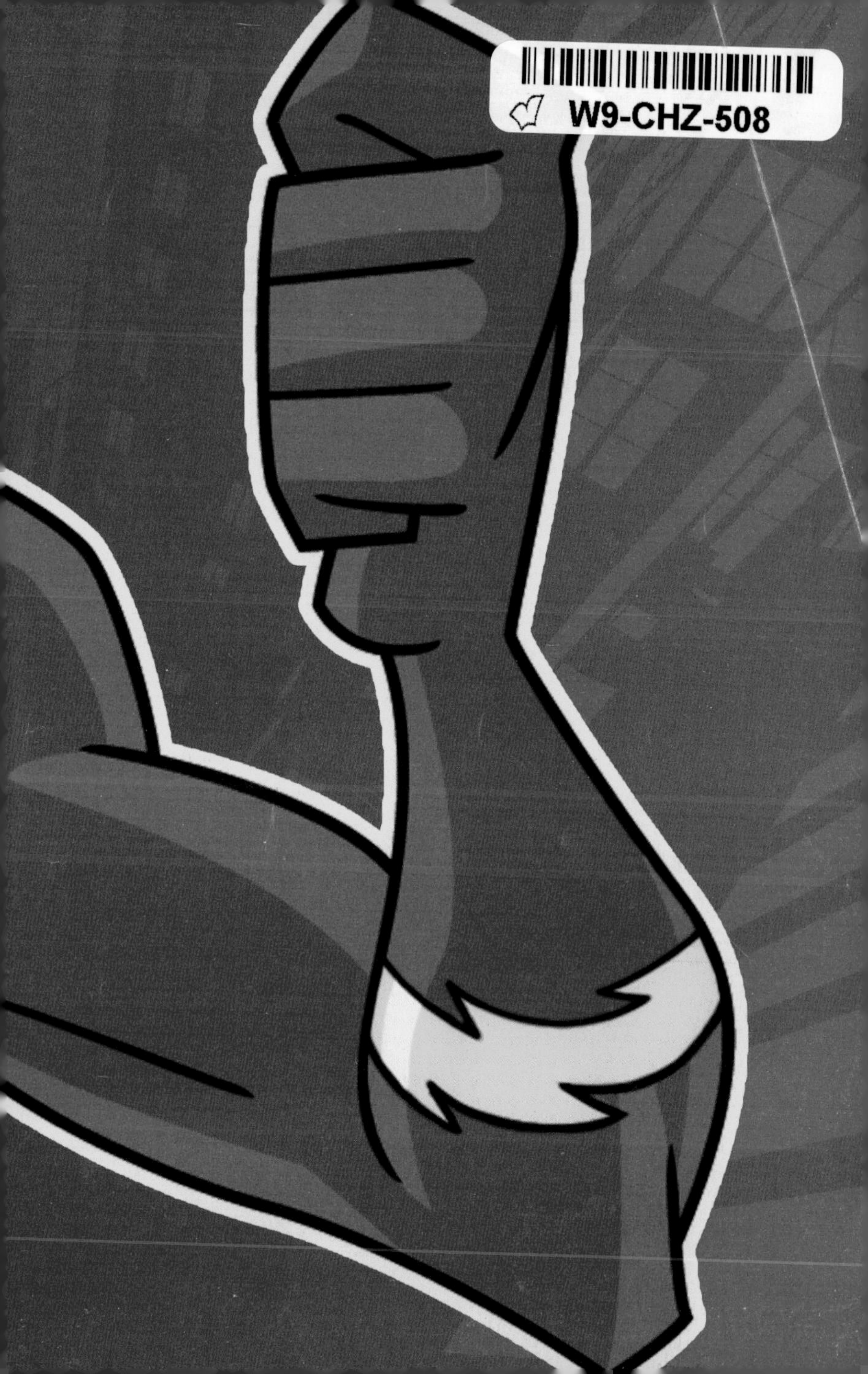

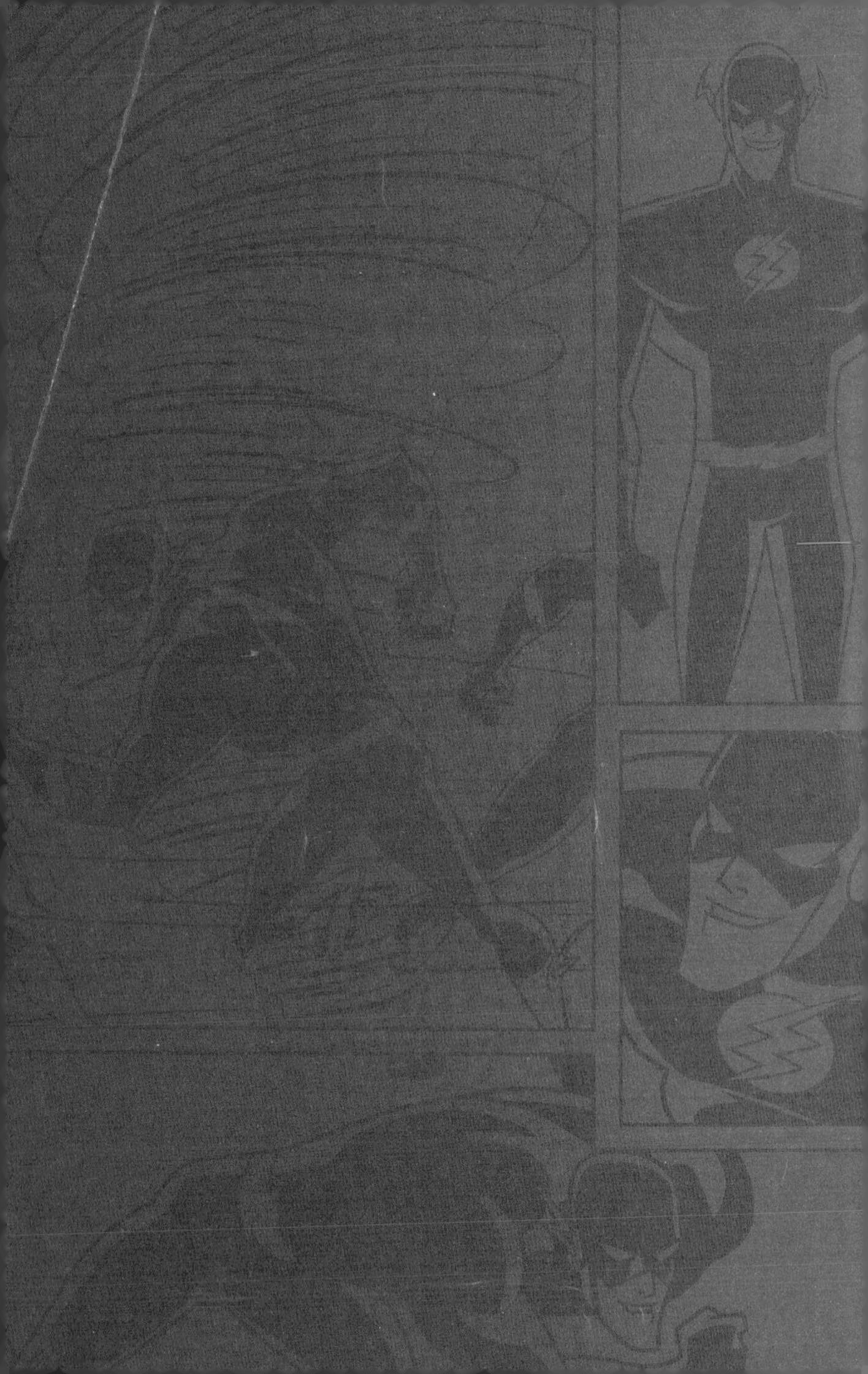

AFTER BEING STRUCK BY A BOLT OF LIGHTNING AND DOUSED WITH CHEMICALS, POLICE SCIENTIST BARRY ALLEN BECAME THE FASTEST MAN ON EARTH . . .

The FLASH

SUPER DC HEROES

WRITTEN BY
BLAKE A. HOENA

ILLUSTRATED BY
ERIK DOESCHER,
MIKE DeCARLO, AND
LEE LOUGHRIDGE

COVER PENCILS BY
DAN SCHOENING

CAPTAIN BOOMERANG'S COMEBACK!

STONE ARCH BOOKS
a capstone imprint

Published by Stone Arch Books in 2012
A Capstone Imprint
151 Good Counsel Drive, P.O. Box 669
Mankato, Minnesota 56002
www.capstonepub.com

STAR25058

Library of Congress Cataloging-in-Publication Data
Hoena, B. A.
  Captain Boomerang's comeback! / written by Blake A. Hoena ; illustrated by
Erik Doescher, Mike DeCarlo and Lee Loughridge.
    p. cm. -- (DC super heroes)
  ISBN-13: 978-1-4342-2625-9 (library binding)
  ISBN-13: 978-1-4342-3411-7 (pbk.)
  1. Flash (Fictitious character)--Juvenile fiction. 2. Superheroes--Juvenile
fiction. 3. Supervillains--Juvenile fiction. 4. Revenge--Juvenile fiction. [1.
Superheroes--Fiction. 2. Supervillains--Fiction. 3. Revenge--Fiction.] I.
Doescher, Erik, ill. II. De Carlo, Mike, ill. III. Loughridge, Lee, ill. IV. Title.
  PZ7.H67127Cap 2012
  813.6--dc22   2011005147

Summary: After a series of random robberies, the Flash's head is whirling at
super-speed. He wants to take down this out-of-sight outlaw, but the confusing
clues aren't adding up. For one man, however, each piece is part of a colossal
comeback. The villain Captain Boomerang is out to seek revenge against
the Scarlet Speedster! But the super hero knows "what goes around, comes
around," and he's not about to let this crazy crook spin out of control.

Art Director: Bob Lentz
Designer: Brann Garvey
Production Specialist: Michelle Biedscheid

Printed in the United States of America in Stevens Point, Wisconsin.
032011
006111WZF11

TABLE of CONTENTS

CHAPTER 1

TEED OFF!

At Central City's famed disc golf course, a blue-and-white disc whizzed through the air. It was sailing in a long, slow arc toward the target on hole number seven. The disc zipped over a small pond. It curved through some pine trees. Then, with a loud **CHING!**, the disc hit metal chains and fell into the target's basket.

Two boys shouted over at the tee box for hole number seven. A tall, gangly man stood there admiring his hole in one.

"Hey, mister!" the boys yelled.

The man turned toward the teens. A dark overcoat hung over his thin shoulders, and a military-looking cap covered his mop of brown hair.

The boys ran up to him. "That was an awesome shot," one boy said as he gave the man a high-five.

"Yeah, I've never seen anyone ace that hole before," the second boy chimed in, also high-fiving the man.

A sinister smirk spread across the man's face. A spark of madness lit his eyes.

"T'was nothing, sports. One and done. That's how I like to play," the man said.

The man then pointed into the distance. "Now, see that truck over there, driving down the road?" he said. "Bet I can hit 'er from here."

The boys turned in the direction the man pointed. An armored truck was driving along the street next to the park.

"No way," one boy exclaimed. "That's, like, 600 feet!"

"Not even the pros could hit a moving target at that distance," the other added.

"Well, watch this, sports," the man said.

He reached under his overcoat and pulled out a metal boomerang.

"Hey, that's not a disc!" one boy said.

Little did the boys know they were talking to Captain Boomerang! The clever super-villain was one of Central City's most devious criminals. Boomerangs were his weapons of choice. "I never said what I'd use to hit it," Captain Boomerang sneered.

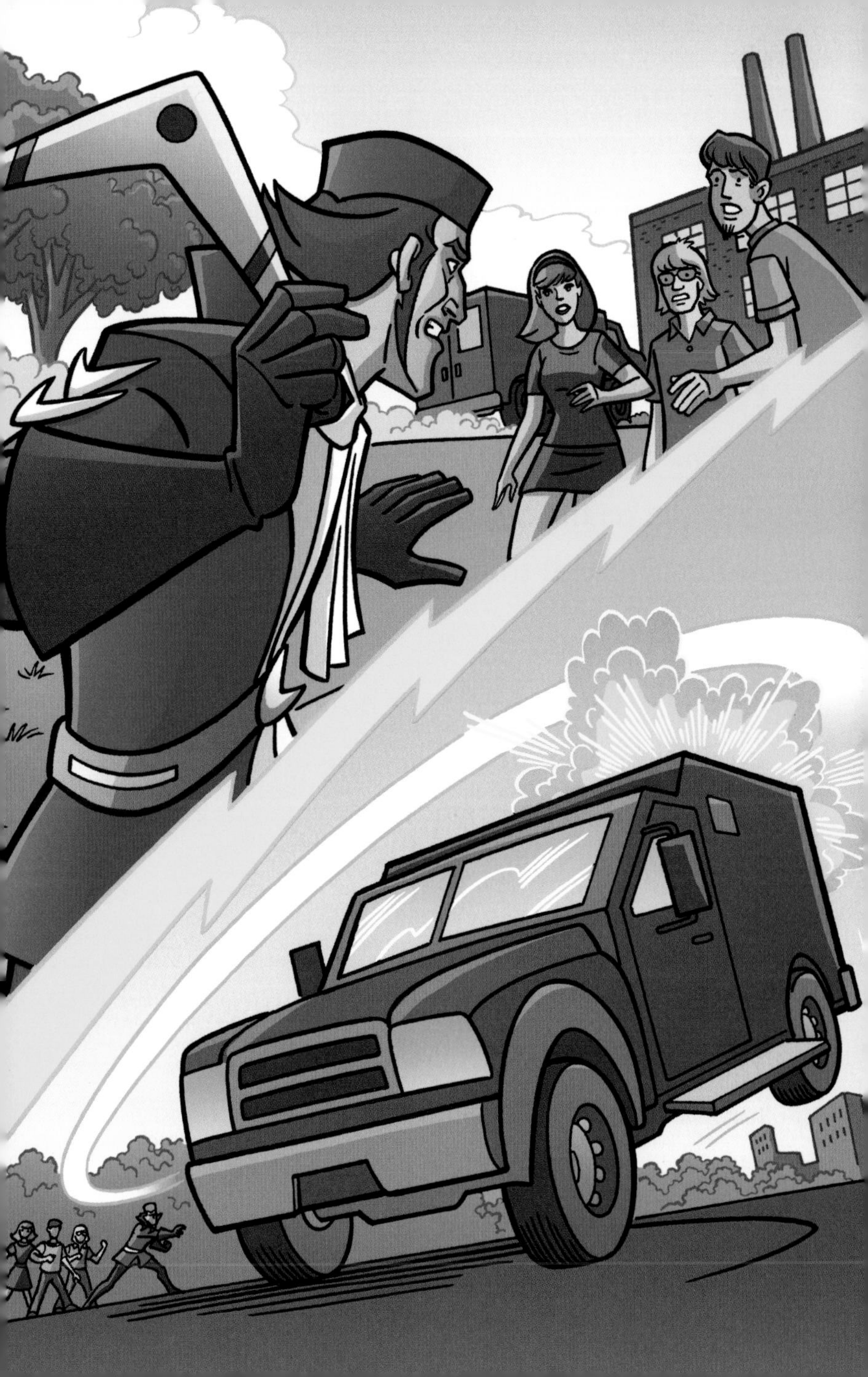

The villain wound up, letting go of the boomerang with a loud grunt. The weapon whooped through the air in a wide arc. The path it followed headed right for the armored truck.

The boys looked at each other in disbelief as the boomerang struck the front of the armored truck and exploded.

KA-BOOM!

The truck skidded to a halt on the park's grass. Sirens wailed. Lights flashed. Two armed guards jumped out of the truck. The boys scattered.

Captain Boomerang casually marched toward the truck. He pulled two more boomerangs from under his jacket. He tossed them at the guards. **THWACK!** The men were knocked out before they knew who was attacking them.

Captain Boomerang then pulled out another boomerang. He tossed it at the truck's front tire. A hiss of air escaped the tire as the boomerang sank into it.

"That'll be a little surprise for the Flash," he said with a chuckle.

*   *   *

Meanwhile, in another part of town, police scientist Barry Allen sat in his lab at police headquarters. He was bored, doodling in a notepad, when the police radio startled him.

"We have a two-eleven in progress near Central City's disc golf course. Assailant is armed with boomerangs . . ." the radio blared. Then, as if answering an unheard question, added, "Yes, I said 'boomerangs!'"

That can only be one man, Barry thought.

Barry knew Captain Boomerang because of his alter ego. Years ago, lightning had struck this very laboratory. The blast bathed Barry with electrically charged chemicals, which gave him the ability to move at super-speed. From that day onward, he was known as the Flash, the Fastest Man Alive, the Scarlet Speedster, or the protector of Central City.

Looking around to make sure no one was watching, Barry flicked a switch on the gold ring he wore. **FWOOOSHHHHHH!!**

Out shot a small red uniform that quickly expanded. In a blur of arms and legs, Barry slipped into the uniform.

Then, faster than a blink of the eye, he turned into a red haze and was gone. He raced through police headquarters faster than anyone could see him.

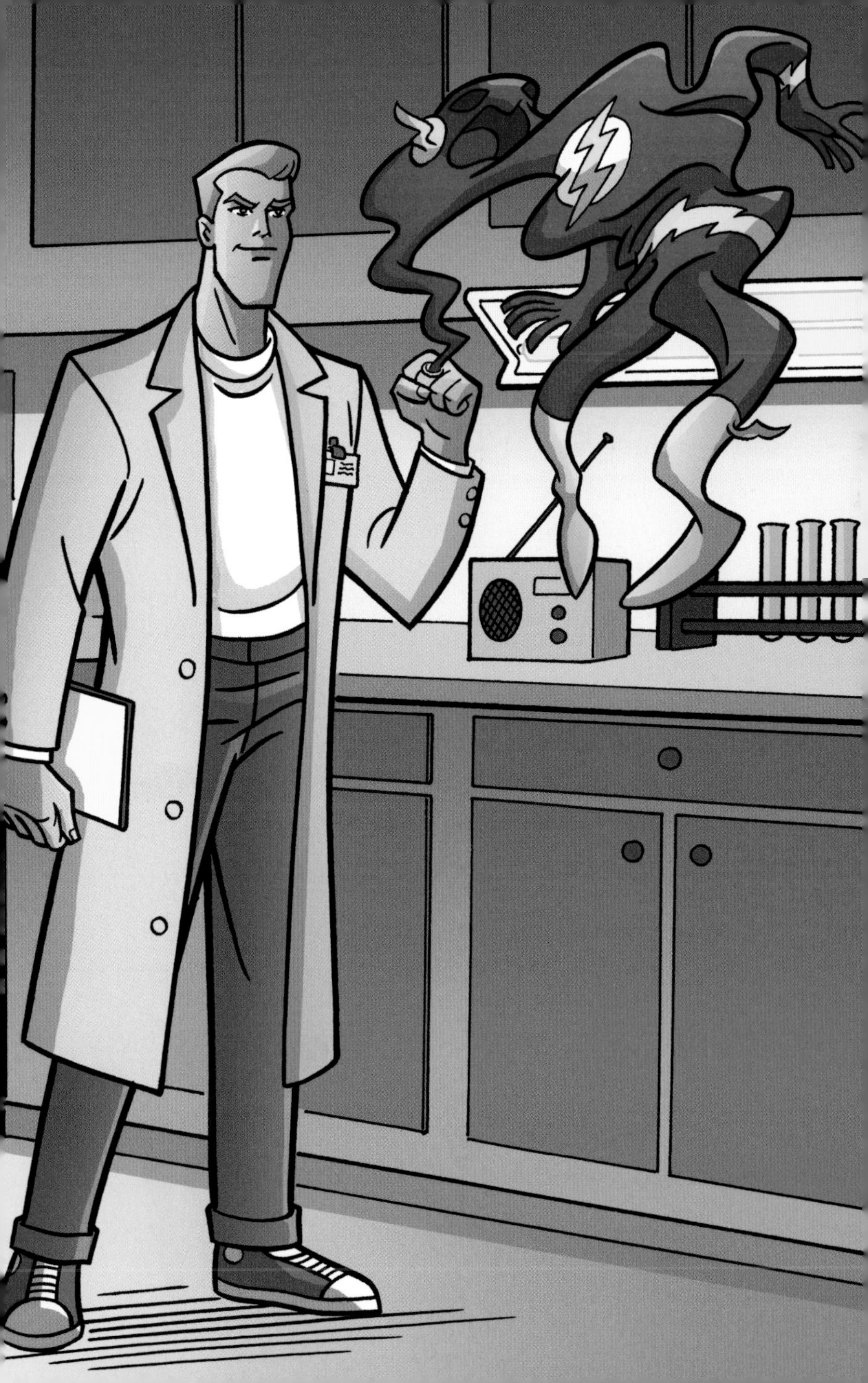

CHAPTER 2

CAUGHT IN A TRAP

Seconds later, the Flash arrived at the disc golf course. Police had set up barriers around the armored trunk to keep back curious spectators.

The Flash examined the back of the armored trunk. The doors hung loosely from their hinges. They looked as if they had been blown open by a small explosive. The side of the truck read "Sparkle's Jewelry Imports."

"What was this truck delivering?" the Flash asked a passing police officer.

"From the driver's logs, it appears a load of rare prism diamonds," the officer answered.

"Were there any boomerangs left behind?" Flash asked, making sure Captain Boomerang had committed the robbery.

"Just one," the policed officer said, waving the Flash over. "It's over here, in the front of the truck."

The Flash walked over and saw the boomerang still stuck in the tire. On it was a small green light.

"It has a power source," said the officer. "We're bringing in a team to inspect it."

The Flash watched the light carefully. Because of his super-speed abilities, he could tell that the light wasn't solid. It was actually blinking very rapidly.

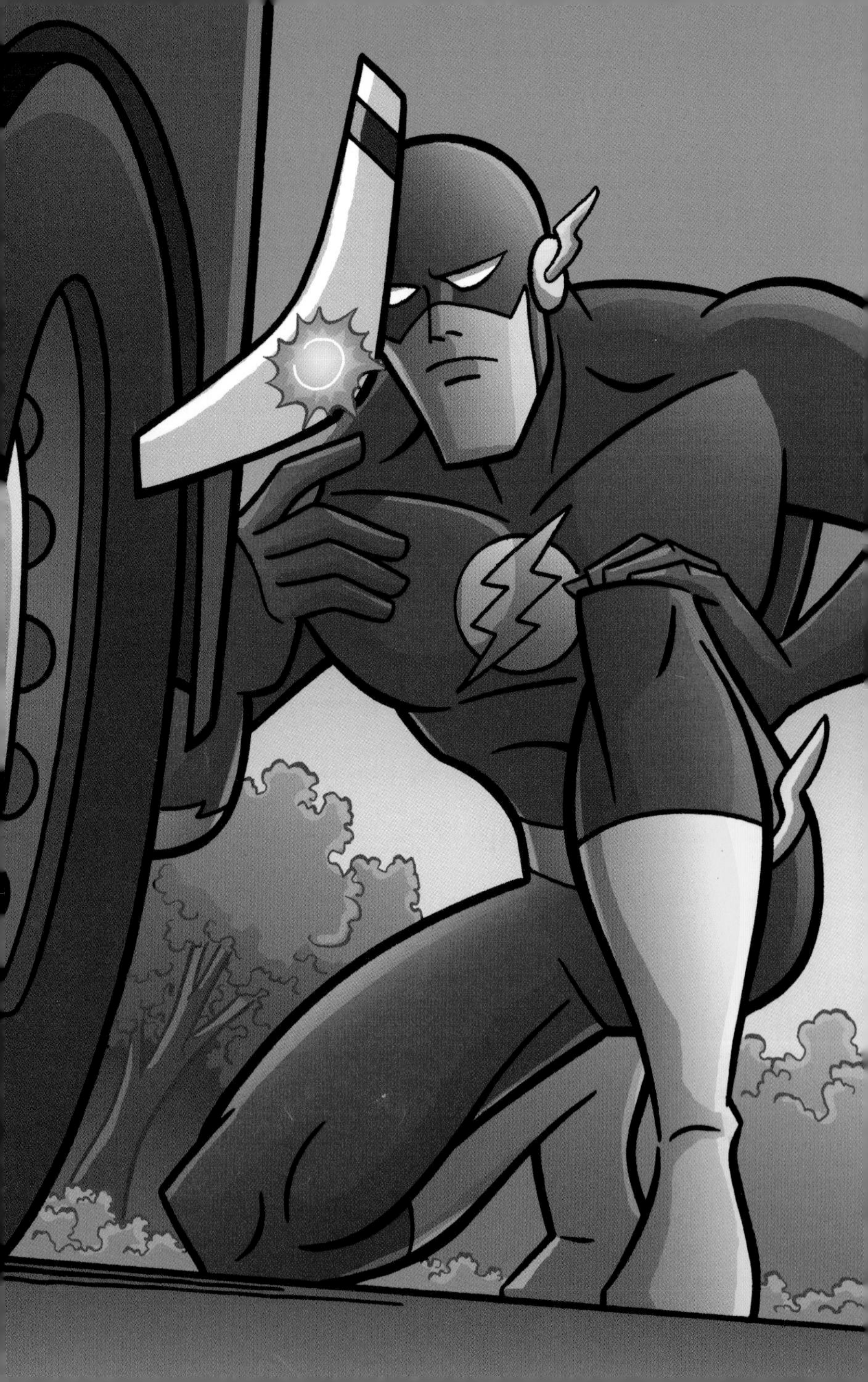

It's a bomb! the thought screamed in his head.

In less than a heartbeat, the Flash scanned the area around him — the crowd, the open park, the truck. There were too many people gathered around and too few places for them to seek cover. He'd have to dispose of the bomb before it went off.

He turned to the police officer. "Evacuate everyone from the area," he said calmly. "It's a bomb."

Before the police officer's look of shock could turn to fear, the Scarlet Speedster knelt beside the front tire of the truck. The blinks were quickly blurring together, which meant the bomb was getting closer to detonation. But the Flash didn't know if he could just yank the boomerang out of the tire or not.

Would that set the bomb off? he wondered.

He never had time to test his theory. Just then, the light turned from green to red.

BARROOOOOMM!!

With his heightened senses, the Flash saw everything as if it moved in slow motion. He watched smoky tendrils reach out from the boomerang as if it were a hungry, fiery beast. People were slogging along, too slow to escape the blast. If he didn't do something quick, the explosion would engulf the crowd, tossing people aside, burning them, or worse.

Faster than the explosion could expand, the Flash moved his hands in a circle. He spun them hundreds of times a second.

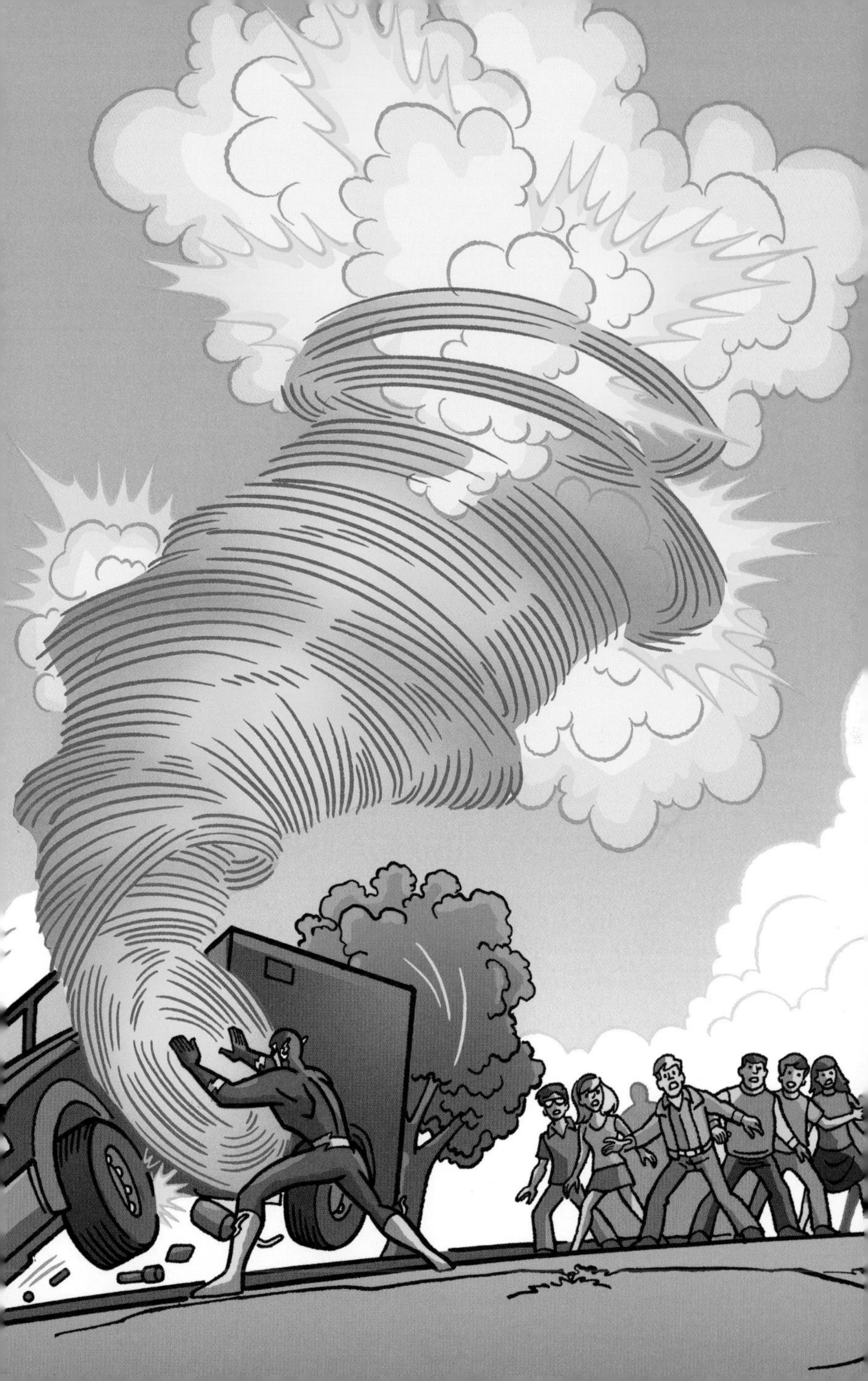

WHOOOOSH!

Flash's circling hands worked like a fan. The motion created a vortex of air that pushed the force of the explosion upward, away from the crowd.

The explosion still knocked people to the street and sent burning pieces of truck high into the air. But no one was seriously hurt.

"It's a good thing you were here," one police officer said to the Flash as he picked himself up off the ground. "Otherwise that bomb could have killed someone."

Yes, thought the Flash, *but I think that bomb was really meant for me.*

*　　*　　*

The next day, Captain Boomerang stumbled out of the warehouse for Homing Devices, Inc.

His clothes were torn and blackened by smoke. Under one arm he held a large sack. Behind him, the doors to the warehouse were scarred by an explosion, and hung loosely from their hinges.

A boy on his bike skidded to a halt in front of Captain Boomerang.

"I heard an explosion!" the boy said. "Are you okay?"

"I'm fine," Captain Boomerang said, pretending to cough. "But there's been a theft. Someone needs to call the cops."

"My dad's over in the park," the boy said. "He's got a cell phone!"

"Then hurry up, kid," Captain Boomerang shouted as the boy sped off on his bike. "Be sure to ask for the Flash's help!"

Once the boy was halfway across the park, Captain Boomerang opened the sack he carried. He scattered its contents in the debris lying in front of the warehouse.

"I sure hope the Flash gets here quick," he said with a laugh. "This will be fun to watch."

CHAPTER 3

PLAYING THE UNFAIR WAY

Barry Allen was sitting in his office. Pieces of the boomerang that had blown up the truck yesterday were scattered across his desk. He was looking for clues in their remains, but had found none.

Then the police radio blared, "There's been a reported robbery in the warehouse district. All cars proceed with caution . . ."

The Flash zoomed out of the lab in his red and gold uniform. He beat the police to the crime scene.

The doors to the warehouse had been blown apart. The hinges still smoked and smoldered. It appeared that whoever broke in had used a small explosive to open the doors. Debris littered the ground.

Before entering the warehouse, the Flash scanned the area. A small crowd had gathered on the street. Police sirens screamed in the distance, yet they were long seconds away. In a park across from the warehouse, a group of people stood, craning their necks skyward. Each held a remote in hand, and they were focused on radio-controlled planes buzzing overhead. A sign in the park read "Remote Control Flight School."

The Flash cautiously walked toward the entrance to the warehouse. He accidentally kicked a shiny piece of debris.

"Ow!" he said. The sharp edge of the metal object nearly cut him. He looked down at his feet. It was not a piece of debris as he had originally thought, but rather a boomerang.

"Captain Boomerang!" the Flash said under his breath.

A green light began flashing on the boomerang. At first, the hero thought it was another bomb, but he noticed that the light blinked at a steady pace. Then, the boomerang began to spin and hover above the ground!

Flash quickly realized it wasn't just one boomerang. There were hundreds of them scattered throughout the debris, all hovering above the ground. Suddenly, the boomerangs began swooping and whirling, diving and looping.

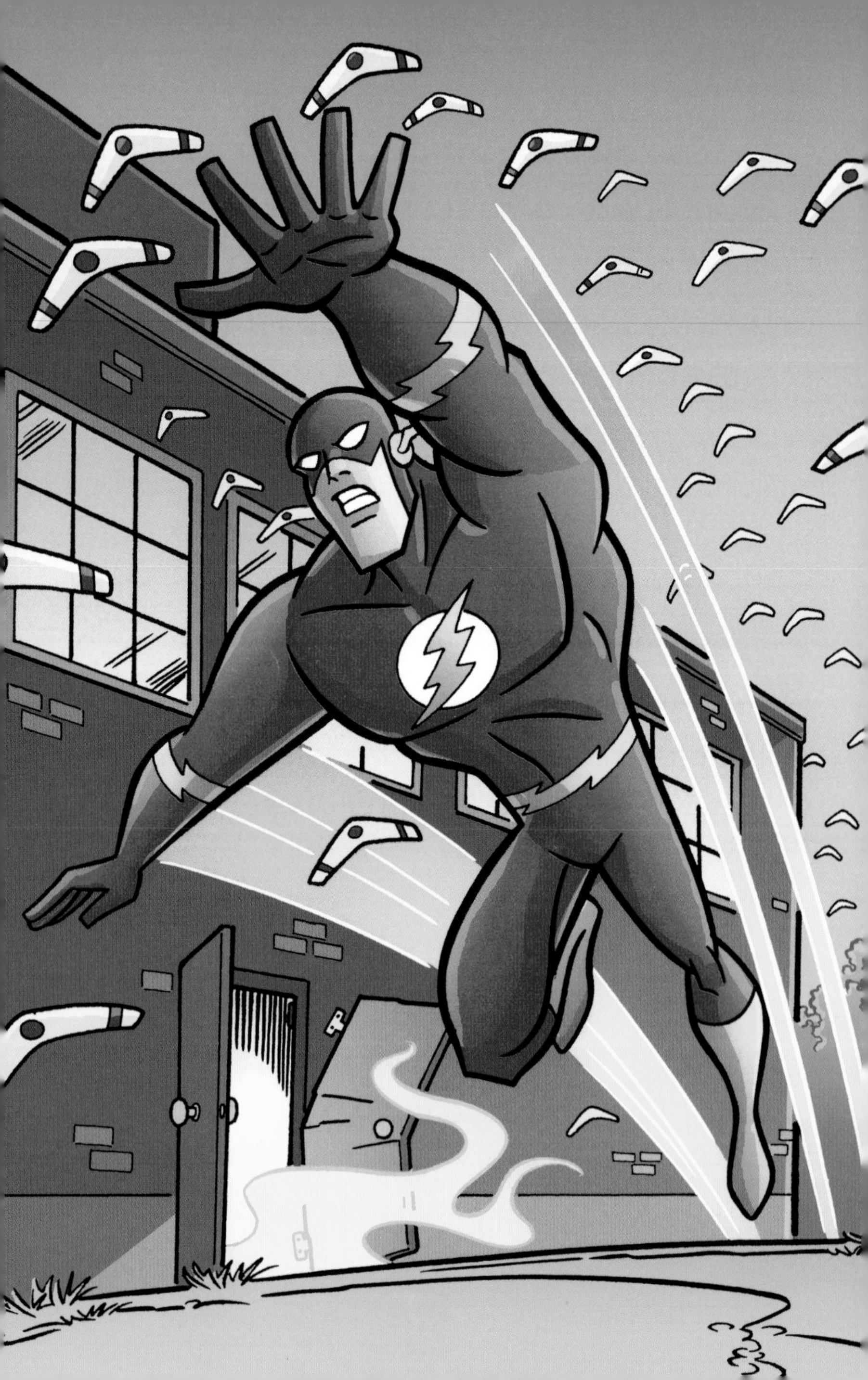

The Flash leaped over a boomerang that darted toward his feet, and then ducked under another as it flew overhead. There was no sense to their crazy flight patterns. The Flash reached out toward a boomerang that was hovering in the air in front of him. Then he pulled back his hand.

The edges of all the boomerangs were razor sharp. The Flash watched one boomerang whirl through a tree. Twigs and leaves flew everywhere as it buzzed through the foliage. Another embedded itself with a heavy *thunk* in a car parked nearby. A third weapon lopped off the top of a street sign.

Faster than thought, the Flash scanned the area. Police cars were nearing. People were screaming and running from the wild whirling weapons.

Flash needed to do something quicker than quick, or people would get hurt.

But what? Flash thought. *It's not possible for me to catch them all.*

Some of the boomerangs flew out of the park and down the street. Others were high overhead. Out of the corner of his eye, Flash saw the people at the flight school. He noticed they seemed utterly confused as they stared up at the sky. They jerked their controllers' joysticks back and forth, and shook them as if something were wrong with the controllers.

Then it dawned on the Flash. There was a connection between the flight students' confusion and the crazily-flying boomerangs. The controllers no longer controlled the planes overhead — they were controlling the boomerangs!

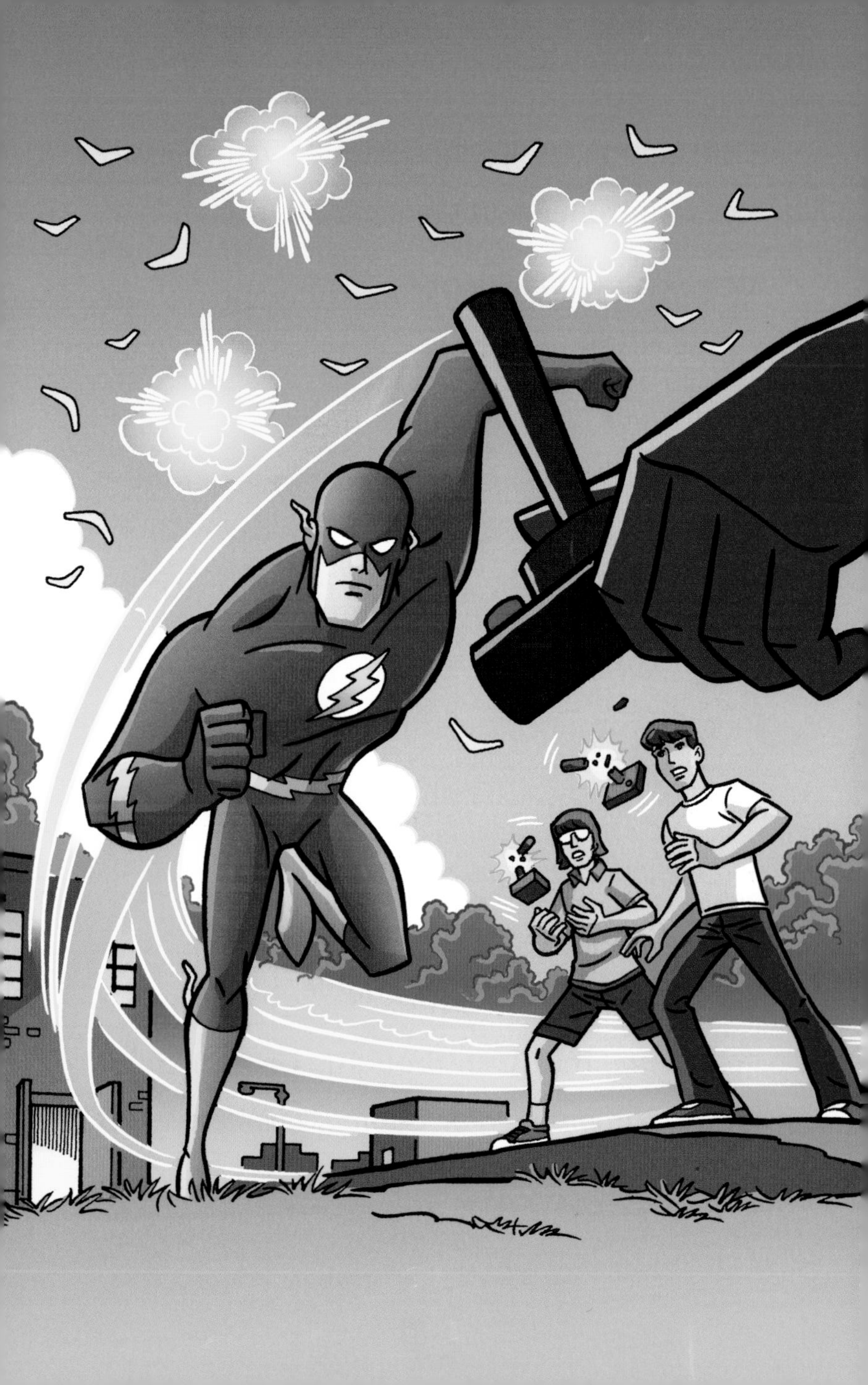

In a blur, the Fastest Man Alive grabbed each controller and smashed it.

As he destroyed each high-tech device, the boomerangs dropped harmlessly from the sky.

Zooming back to the warehouse, the Flash approached a police officer who was looking through the building.

"Do you know if anything was stolen?" the Flash asked.

"Some electronic equipment," she replied. "Nothing too valuable, I think."

Hmmm, the Flash thought. *That's two robberies committed by Captain Boomerang. But what's their connection?*

*　　*　　*

The very next day, Captain Boomerang was seen rushing out of Gizmos and Gadgets — a high-tech electronics store on the first floor of the Central City mall. A cloud of smoke trailed behind him.

As he left the store, people milled about.

"What happened?" they asked. "Are you hurt?"

"I'm fine, mates. Just dandy," Captain Boomerang wheezed, acting as if he were hurt. "But somebody call the police. There's been a robbery. If the Flash gets here quick, maybe he can catch the thief."

And then he was gone, disappearing into the crowd.

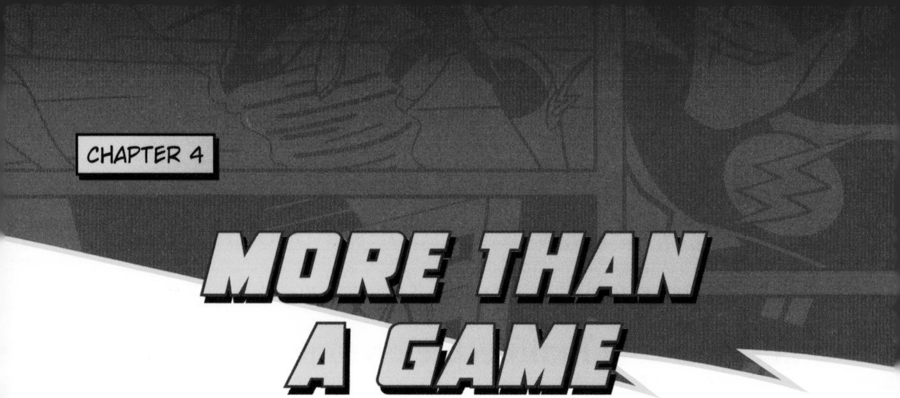

CHAPTER 4

MORE THAN A GAME

As soon as Barry heard about the robbery on his police radio, he left in a flash. He was a red blur, speeding through town, racing toward the mall.

After two booby-trapped crime scenes, the Flash was very cautious as he entered the mall. The glass doors to the electronics store had been shattered by a small explosion. Sirens blared. Glass shards and strips of metal from the store's display cases littered the floor. Inside the store sat a large metal box in the middle of the room.

It was the only thing that did not look as if it had been damaged by the break-in.

The robber must have left it behind, Barry thought. *It was probably Captain Boomerang, again.*

Warily, the Flash approached the box. As he did, a green light on the top of it began to blink.

Uh-oh, he thought. *I'd better be prepared for anything.*

The lid to the box popped open and small, quarter-sized boomerangs flew out, whirling and swirling about. As one of the boomerangs hit the ceiling, it exploded.

BOOM! Then another hit the wall and exploded. **BOOM!** Soon, the Flash was dodging dozens of boomerangs — and still more were bursting from the box!

As the number of explosions increased, the Flash could sense the building around him weakening. If this continued, the building could collapse with hundreds of people inside. He had to do something fast!

But what? Flash thought.

There were hundreds of the tiny boomerangs now. He could try catching them before they hit something, but they might explode in his hands. He couldn't get near the box to close the lid because the swarm of boomerangs spinning around it was too thick. He needed to lure the boomerangs out of the mall.

The Flash began flailing his arm in a circle. He was forcing the air out of the area in front of him and creating a vacuum. As he did this, the tiny boomerangs began to loop in his direction.

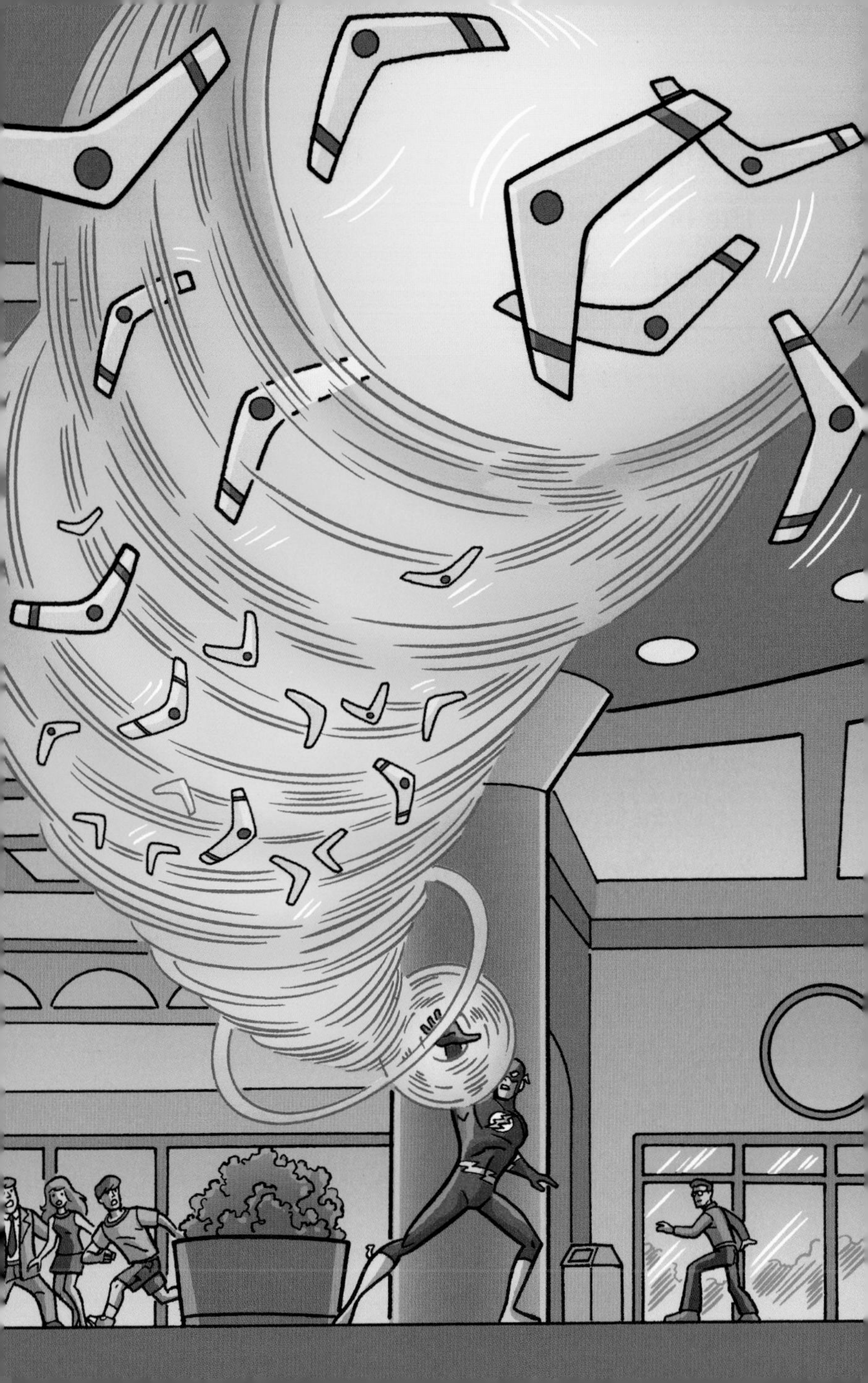

He worked slowly at first, making sure the boomerangs were being sucked into the vacuum he was creating. Then the Flash began to back out of the store.

WHOOOOSH!

The Flash sped off down the mall's wide hallway and out its double doors. The swarm of tiny boomerangs trailed behind him. Some flew off and hit walls, some collided with each other and exploded, but most were sucked outside.

Then the Scarlet Speedster sped through town. The vacuum of his spinning arms dragged the swarm of boomerangs behind him.

Once he reached a desolate area, he stopped. The remaining boomerangs either landed and exploded or crashed into each other harmlessly.

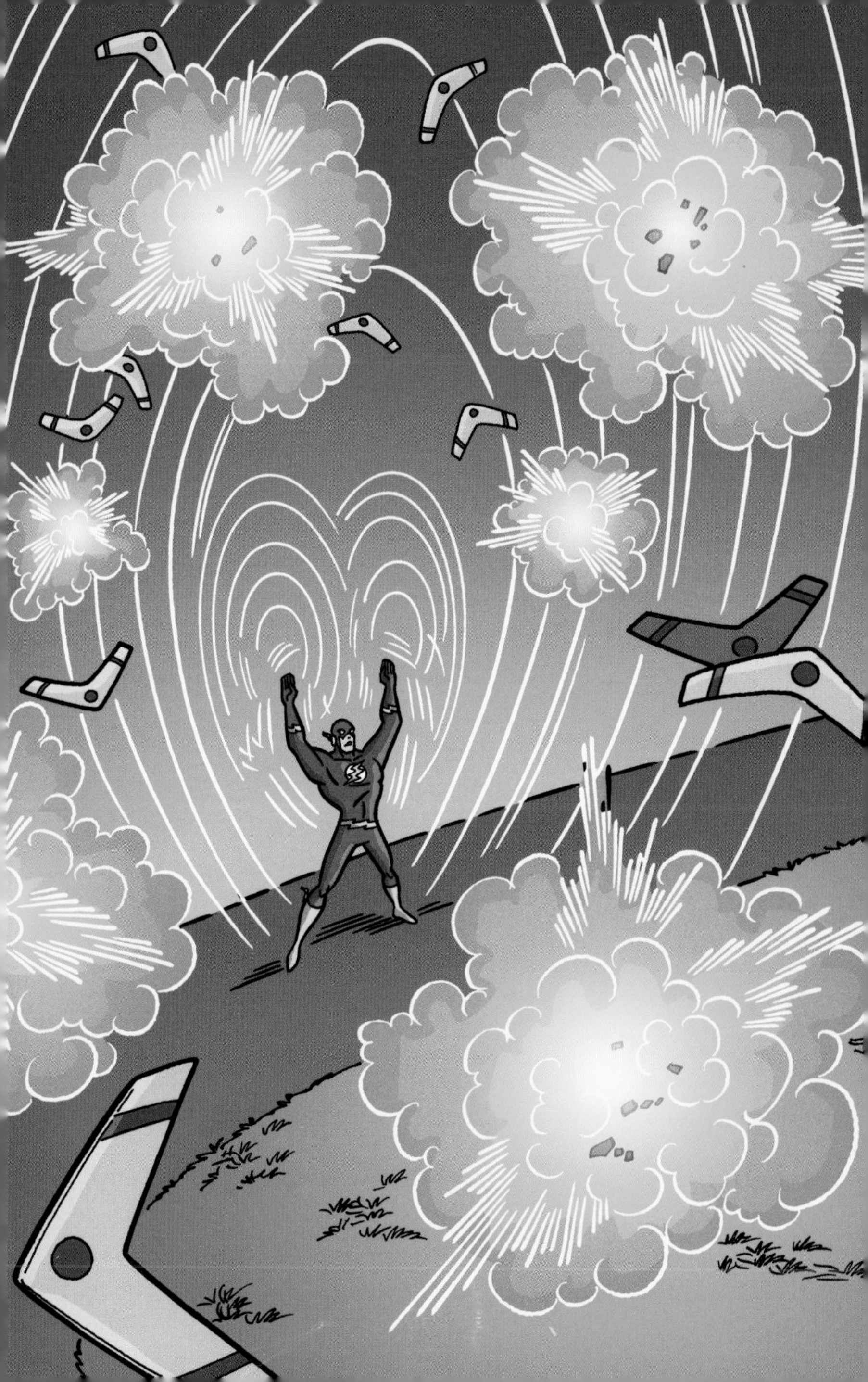

Later that day, Barry Allen sat in his lab. He was perplexed. So far, three crimes had been committed — all by Captain Boomerang. He listed them in his notepad:

1. An armored truck carrying diamonds

2. Homing devices from a warehouse

3. High-tech electronics from a computer store

His mind sorted through hundreds of possible connections, but no explanation he could think of made any sense.

Why did Captain Boomerang steal these items? Barry wondered. Then his mind turned to the events that occurred after he had arrived at the crime scenes. Each time, there was a surprise waiting for the Flash, and the traps didn't spring *until* he arrived.

The thing that confused Barry the most was that he hadn't seen Captain Boomerang trying to escape any of the crime scenes. No matter how fast Flash had arrived, the villain was nowhere to be seen. And in the case of the last two crimes, he had arrived only moments after the crimes had been committed.

That left only two possibilities. Either Captain Boomerang was faster than the Fastest Man Alive, or he had never even left the crime scenes.

Barry knew which possibility was most likely — Captain Boomerang had been there, waiting for the Flash the whole time! *That explains why the traps were sprung just as I was about to investigate the crime scenes,* Barry thought. Now all he needed to do was test his theory at the next robbery.

*   *   *

Captain Boomerang stumbled out of the Central City's Modern Arts Museum. A cloud of smoke followed him out the door. He collided with a group of surprised summer school students who were on a field trip. A sign above the museum's doors read *Van Gogh Exhibit*.

"What happened?" the students asked. "Are you okay?"

"I'm fine, mates," Captain Boomerang said, rubbing his head as if he were hurt. "But I think some thieves stole a valuable painting."

The students looked horrified.

Captain Boomerang urged the students' teachers, "Call the police, quick!"

As the police were being called, Captain Boomerang vanished into the crowd that had gathered around the entrance to the museum. Once he had weaved his way through the people, he walked halfway down the street. He entered a narrow alley, then climbed a fire escape to the top of a building.

He waited. He knew the Flash would be here soon to fall into another one of his traps. *And this one is even more dangerous than the rest!* he thought.

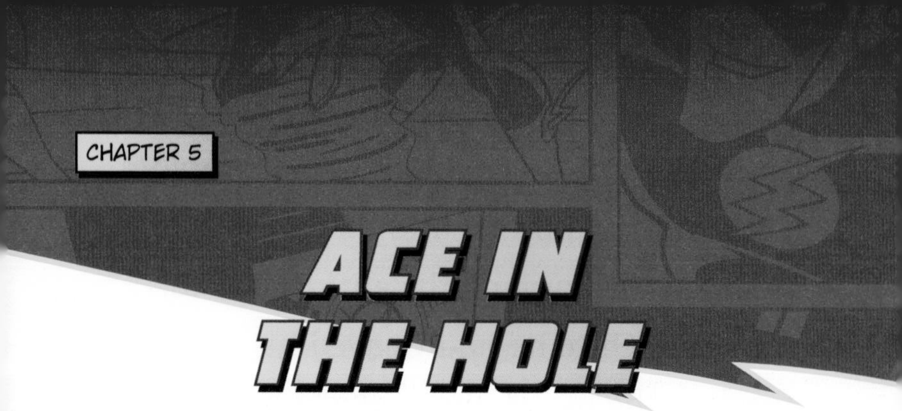

CHAPTER 5

ACE IN THE HOLE

As soon as he heard the police radio announce the location of the theft, the Flash was on his way to the museum. When he arrived, he didn't stop to investigate like he had the last three times. Instead, he raced around, faster than anyone could see. If Captain Boomerang couldn't see Flash, then he couldn't set off the trap as he had done at the previous crime scenes.

First, the Flash sped through the museum looking for Captain Boomerang.

There was no sign of him. Only police officers were in the building now. Flash raced through the crowd outside. All people noticed was a sudden gust of wind as the super hero sped by them. But again, no sign of Captain Boomerang.

As he ran, the Flash scanned the area. If Captain Boomerang wasn't watching in the museum or in the crowd that had gathered around the museum, then he had to be watching from above.

One by one, the Flash checked the buildings overlooking the museum. He zoomed from window to window. He raced up fire escapes to the rooftops, and then down again.

After checking a dozen buildings, he finally spotted Captain Boomerang at the top of a fire escape.

The Flash zoomed up behind him. "It's time for you to take a trip back to Iron Heights Penitentiary," the Flash said.

Captain Boomerang slowly spun around toward his nemesis. In one hand, he held a rolled-up painting. The other hand appeared to be clutching air.

"You're getting slow, mate," Captain Boomerang sneered. "It took you until my fourth crime to catch up to me. And I bet you still haven't even figured out the purpose of my thefts."

"It doesn't matter now," the Flash said. "You're going to jail, and that painting is going back to the museum."

"Oh, *this*?" Captain Boomerang said with a laugh. "I just fancied it. It'll look nice hanging in my bathroom."

The villain smiled wickedly. "Now let me show you what I've been up to."

Captain Boomerang made a throwing motion with his empty hand. The Flash didn't see him holding anything, so he didn't move. Suddenly, something thudded against his shoulder, and the Flash fell.

"Ha! Didn't see that one coming, did you, mate?" Captain Boomerang said, laughing. "I used prism diamonds to create an invisible boomerang. The diamonds bend light so that you can't see the boomerang coming!"

Captain Boomerang pulled an object from his coat. He lifted a shiny disc over his head. "This isn't one of my ordinary boomerangs," he said. "This uses the high-tech gadgetry I stole. I call it my Disc of Death!"

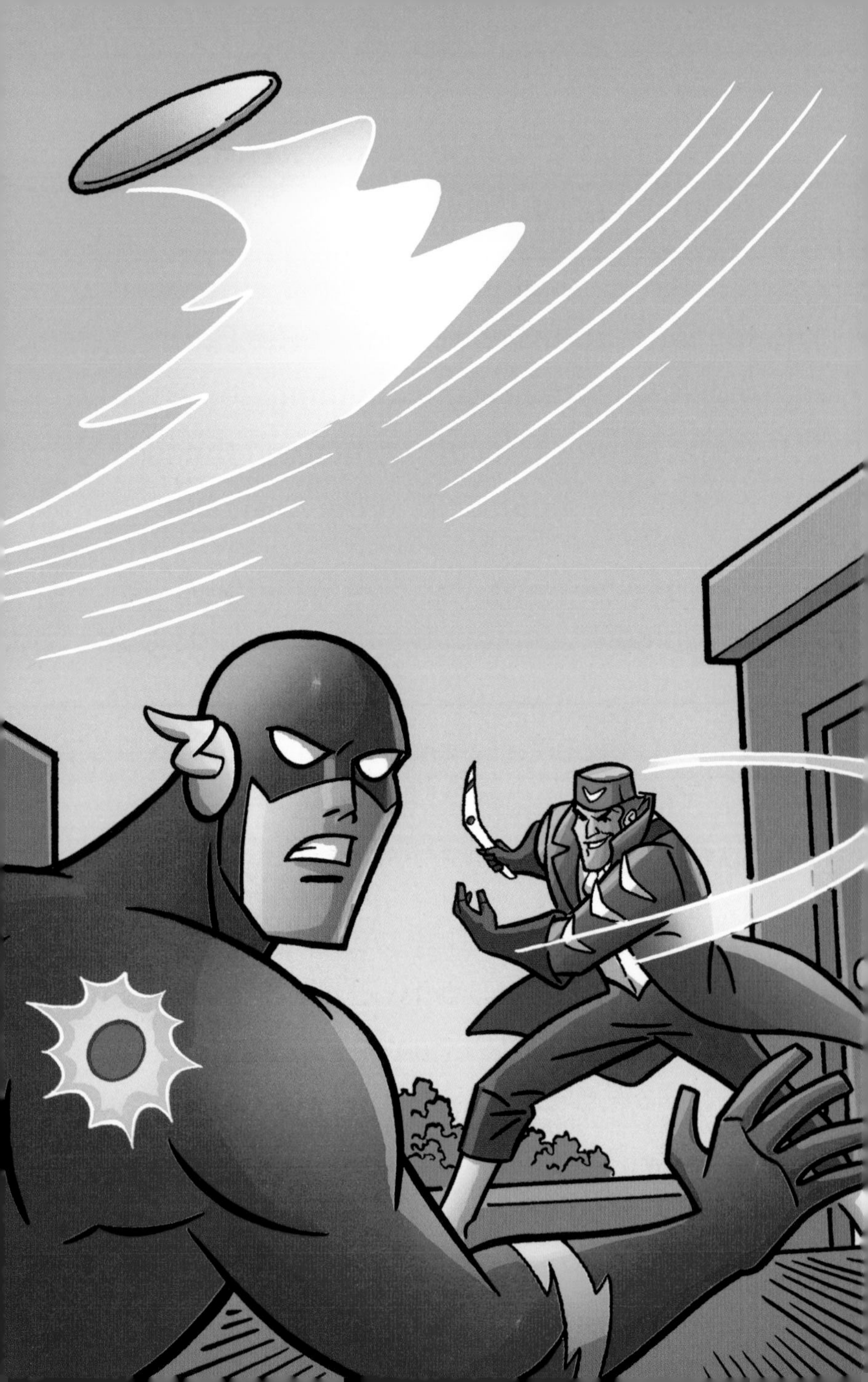

Flash leaped to his feet as Captain Boomerang tossed the disc. **ZING!** It quickly buzzed toward him, but the hero easily dodged it.

"You missed," the Flash said.

"Did I?" Captain Boomerang replied.

Uh oh, the Flash thought. He turned around just as the disc came buzzing back at him. He wasn't quick enough to avoid it, and the edge of the disc cut his arm.

"Ow!" the Flash shouted.

"And it's razor sharp, too!" Captain Boomerang said. **HAHAHAHA!**

The disc spun back around and whirled after the Flash. The Scarlet Speedster was a red blur of limbs as he tried to avoid the whirling metal.

"Oh yeah, one more thing, Flash," Captain Boomerang said. "I've designed my Disc of Death not only to track its target, but to be nearly as fast as you!"

The Flash didn't have enough room to maneuver on top of the building. The disc was also incredibly fast, so he couldn't just run away. The disc's razor-sharp edges zoomed and buzzed past him at a maddening pace. He soon had nicks and cuts from too many close calls.

Why can't I lose this thing? Flash wondered. *I'm still faster than it is, but I can't seem to shake it!*

As he zoomed about, the Flash felt an odd sensation. There was a small amount of drag on his uniform. He felt the wind resistance in the spot where the stealth boomerang had hit him.

Feeling around his shoulder, he found a small object attached to his uniform. *A homing device!* the Flash thought. *If I pull it off, I could escape this dreaded disc.*

But it was stuck to his uniform. And now, the Scarlet Speedster was trapped. He stood, balancing precariously, on the edge of the building's roof with the disc swooping down on him. A hundred possible escapes were racing through his mind, but none of them would shake this thing.

I've got it! the Flash thought.

The hero sped up his body's molecules. When the disc swooped in for the kill, it harmlessly phased through his body — and his specially designed uniform.

But the disc did hit *something*. The Flash heard a metal **CLANK!**

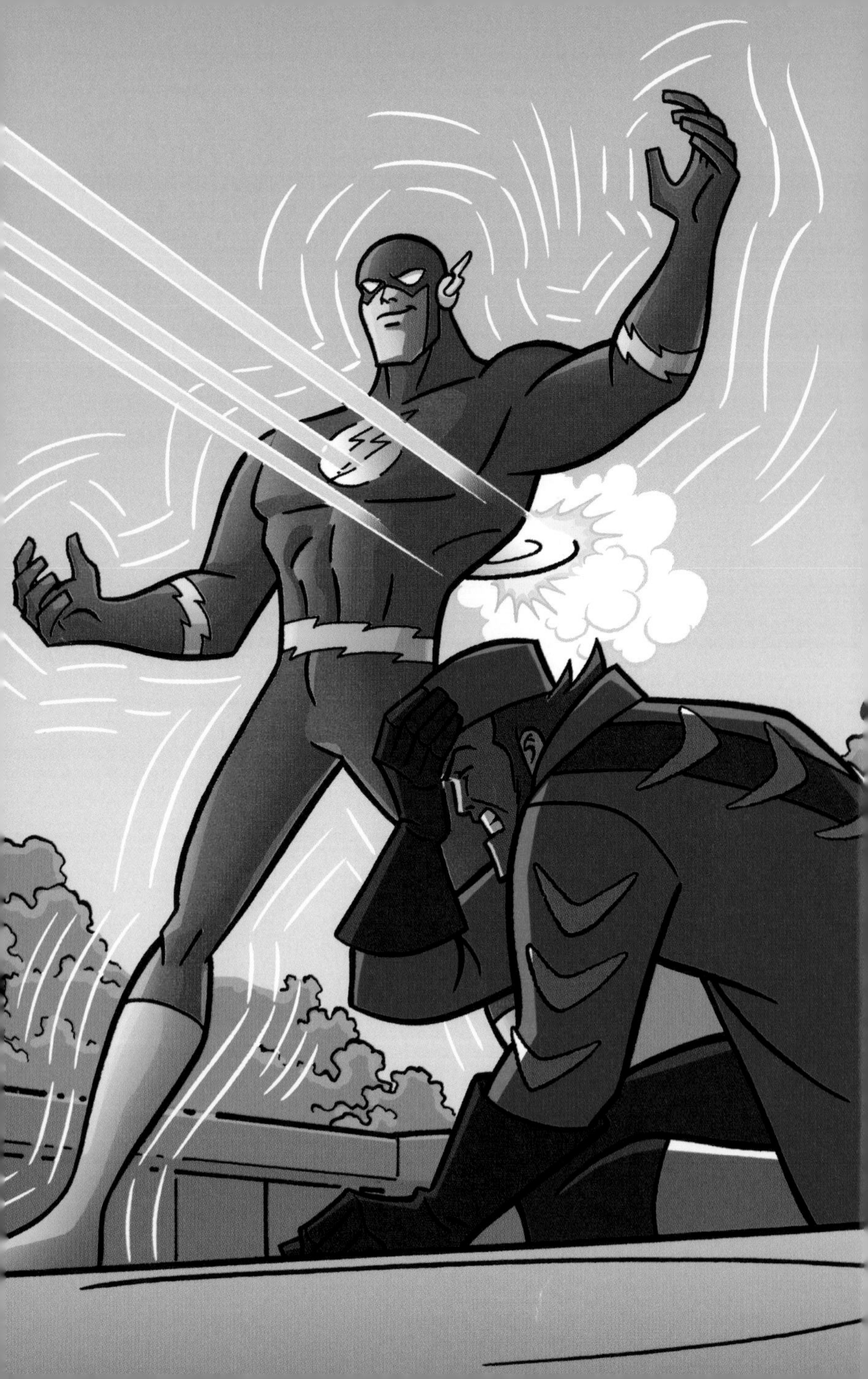

The disc homed in on the device attached to his uniform and sliced it in two! With the homing device destroyed, the Disc of Death fell harmlessly to the ground.

"I, um, I —" Captain Boomerang stammered.

"Speechless, Captain Boomerang?" the Flash said, grinning. "I guess that's the difference between discs and boomerangs. Discs aren't known for their *comebacks*."

The Flash grabbed Captain Boomerang by the arm and led him to the fire escape. Two police officers were just climbing onto the roof. They took Captain Boomerang into custody.

"You'll have time to think of your own in prison," the Flash said as the officers led his nemesis away.

File Edit View Go Window Help

CAPTAIN BOOMERANG

CAPTAIN BOOMERANG

REAL NAME: GEORGE "DIGGER" HARKNESS

OCCUPATION: CRIMINAL

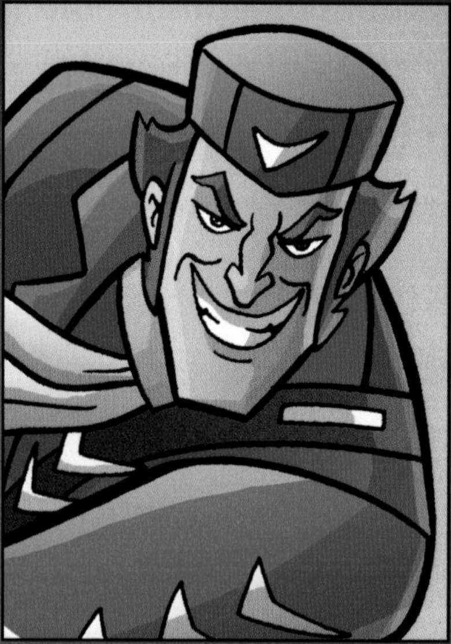

HEIGHT: 5' 9"

WEIGHT: 167 LBS.

EYES: BROWN

HAIR: BROWN

SPECIAL POWERS/ABILITIES:

Boomerang-throwing specialist and an expert marksman; engineers numerous boomerangs to use as deadly weapons.

done

CAPTAIN BOOMERANG BIO

BIOGRAPHY:

Born in Australia, George "Digger" Harkness enjoyed throwing wooden boomerangs as a child. As a teenager, Harkness moved to the United States, and his love for the toy traveled with him. He acquired a job at the Wiggins Game Company, demonstrating boomerangs for customers and their children. Soon, however, the low-paying job couldn't support his upper-class desires. He began a life of crime, engineering deadly boomerangs for use as weapons.

CAPTAIN BOOMERANG FACTS

W.W. "Walt" Wiggins, owner of Wiggins Game Company, was Captain Boomerang's father.

Captain Boomerang is a member of the Rogues' Gallery — villains set on defeating the Flash.

Captain Boomerang nearly destroyed the Flash by sending him to space on a giant boomerang.

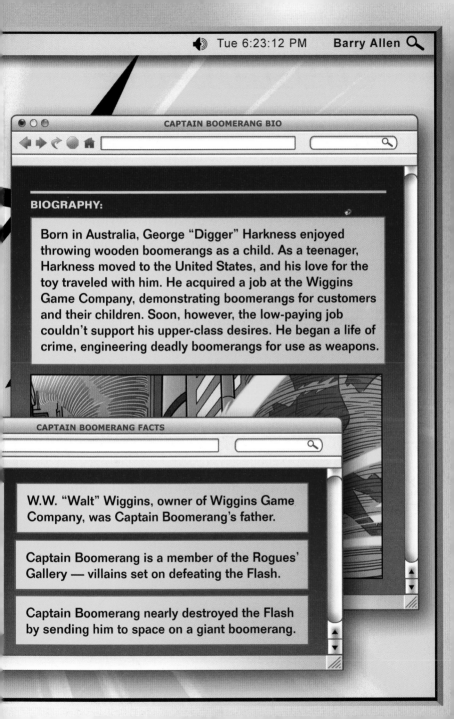

BIOGRAPHIES

Blake A. Hoena grew up in central Wisconsin, where, in his youth, he wrote stories about trolls lumbering around in the woods behind his parent's house. Later, he moved to Minnesota to pursue a Masters of Fine Arts degree in Creative Writing from Minnesota State University, Mankato. Since graduating, Blake has written more than forty books for children.

Erik Doescher is a freelance illustrator based in Dallas, Texas. He attended the School of Visual Arts in New York City. Erik illustrated for a number of comic studios throughout the 1990s, and then moved to Texas to pursue videogame development and design. However, he has not given up on illustrating his favorite comic book characters.

Mike DeCarlo is a longtime contributor of comic art whose range extends from Batman and Iron Man to Bugs Bunny and Scooby-Doo. He resides in Connecticut with his wife and four children.

Lee Loughridge has been working in comics for more than fifteen years. He currently lives in sunny California in a tent on the beach.

GLOSSARY

booby trap (BOO-bee TRAP)—a type of trap triggered when a victim disturbs a seemingly harmless object

debris (duh-BREE)—the scattered pieces of something that has been broken or destroyed

devious (DEE-vee-uhss)—tricky, deceptive, or unable to be trusted

disc golf (DISK GOLF)—a game in which players throw plastic discs around a special course and into a target basket

nemesis (NEH-muh-sis)—a rival or opponent

prism (PRIZ-uhm)—a clear glass shape that bends light or breaks it up into different colors; a prism usually has a triangular base.

sinister (SIN-uh-stur)—seeming evil and threatening

theory (THEER-ee)—an idea or opinion based on some fact or evidence but not proved

vortex (VOHR-teks)—something that resembles a whirlpool, such as swirling air or water

DISCUSSION QUESTIONS

1. Which of Captain Boomerang's gadgets was your favorite? Why?

2. The Flash uses his super-speed to protect Central City. If you had super-speed, what would you do with it? Discuss your answers.

3. Captain Boomerang is a boomerang-throwing expert. If you could be an expert at anything, what would you choose? Why?

WRITING PROMPTS

1. Captain Boomerang likes to collect boomerangs. Do you have a favorite thing to collect? Write about the reasons you enjoy it so much.

2. Create your own high-tech boomerang. Describe its powers and give your boomerang a name. Then draw a picture of the souped-up toy.

3. Imagine you could run as fast as the Flash. Where would you go? What places would you see? Write about having super-speed for a day!

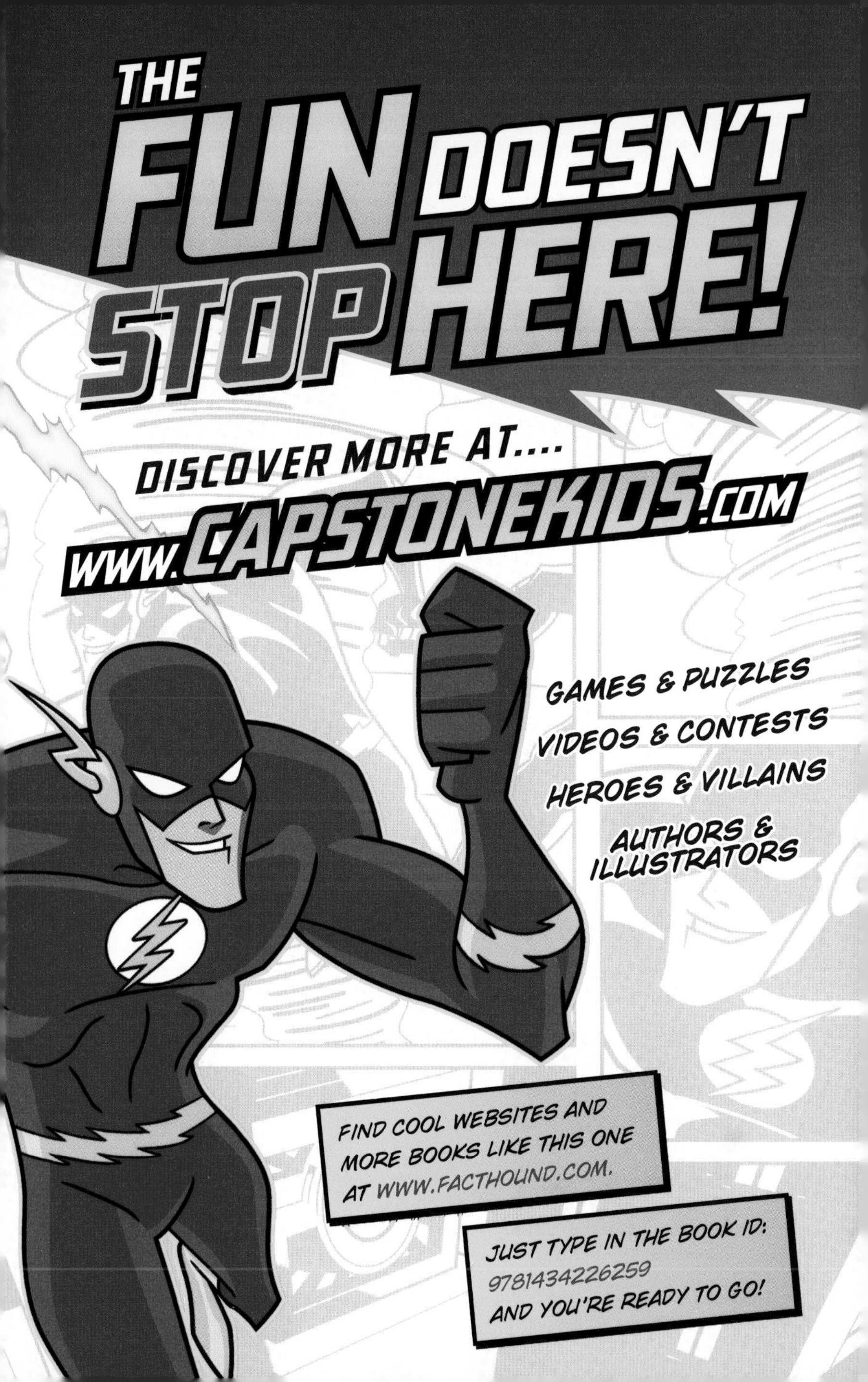
THE FUN DOESN'T STOP HERE!
DISCOVER MORE AT....
WWW.CAPSTONEKIDS.COM
GAMES & PUZZLES
VIDEOS & CONTESTS
HEROES & VILLAINS
AUTHORS & ILLUSTRATORS
FIND COOL WEBSITES AND MORE BOOKS LIKE THIS ONE AT WWW.FACTHOUND.COM.
JUST TYPE IN THE BOOK ID: 9781434226259 AND YOU'RE READY TO GO!

MORE NEW The FLASH ADVENTURES!

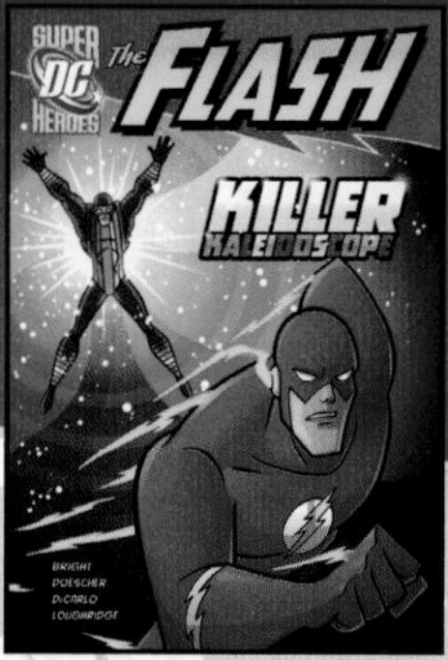
SUPER DC HEROES
The FLASH
KILLER KALEIDOSCOPE
BRIGHT
DOESCHER
DECARLO
LOUGHRIDGE

KILLER KALEIDOSCOPE

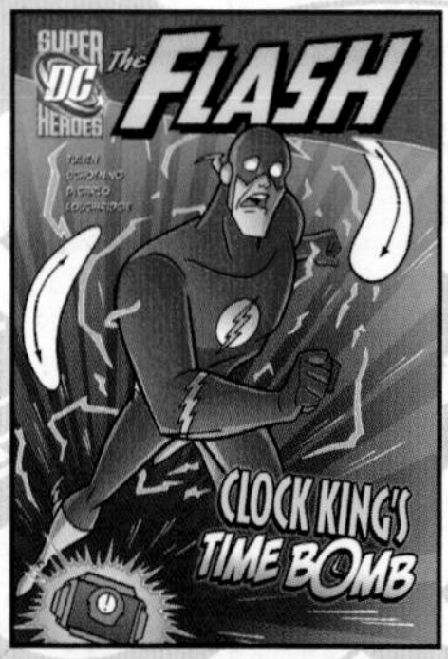
SUPER DC HEROES
The FLASH
CLOCK KING'S TIME BOMB

CLOCK KING'S TIME BOMB

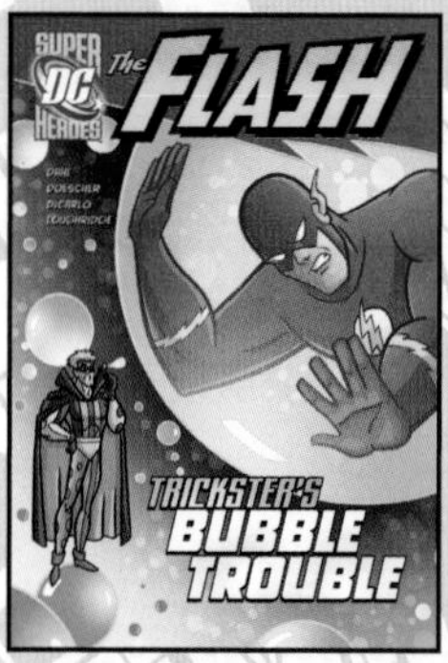
SUPER DC HEROES
The FLASH
TRICKSTER'S BUBBLE TROUBLE

TRICKSTER'S BUBBLE TROUBLE

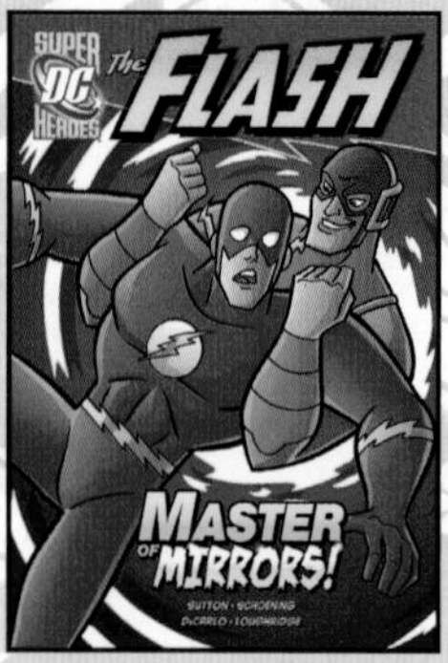
SUPER DC HEROES
The FLASH
MASTER OF MIRRORS!

MASTER OF MIRRORS!

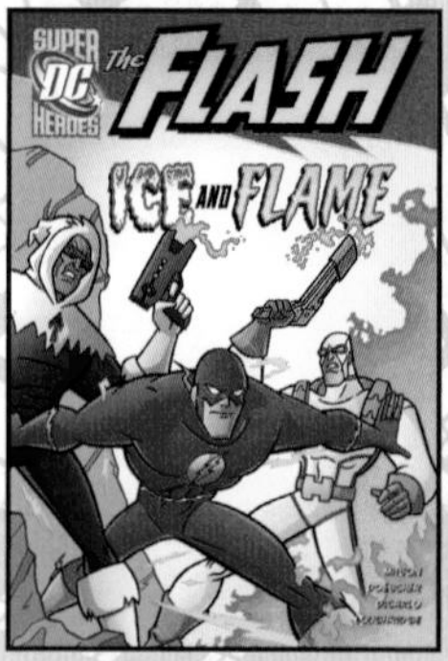
SUPER DC HEROES
The FLASH
ICE AND FLAME

ICE AND FLAME

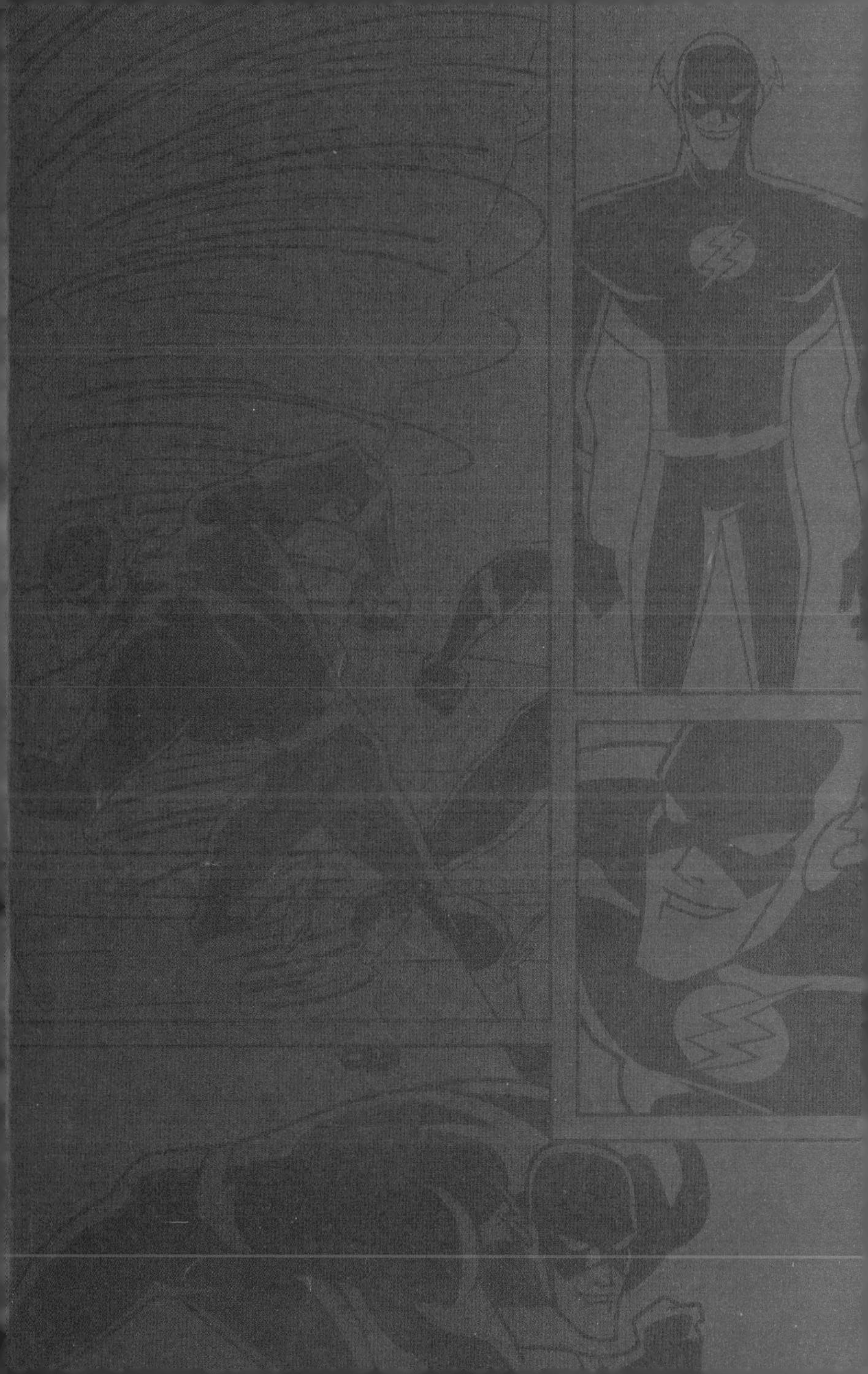

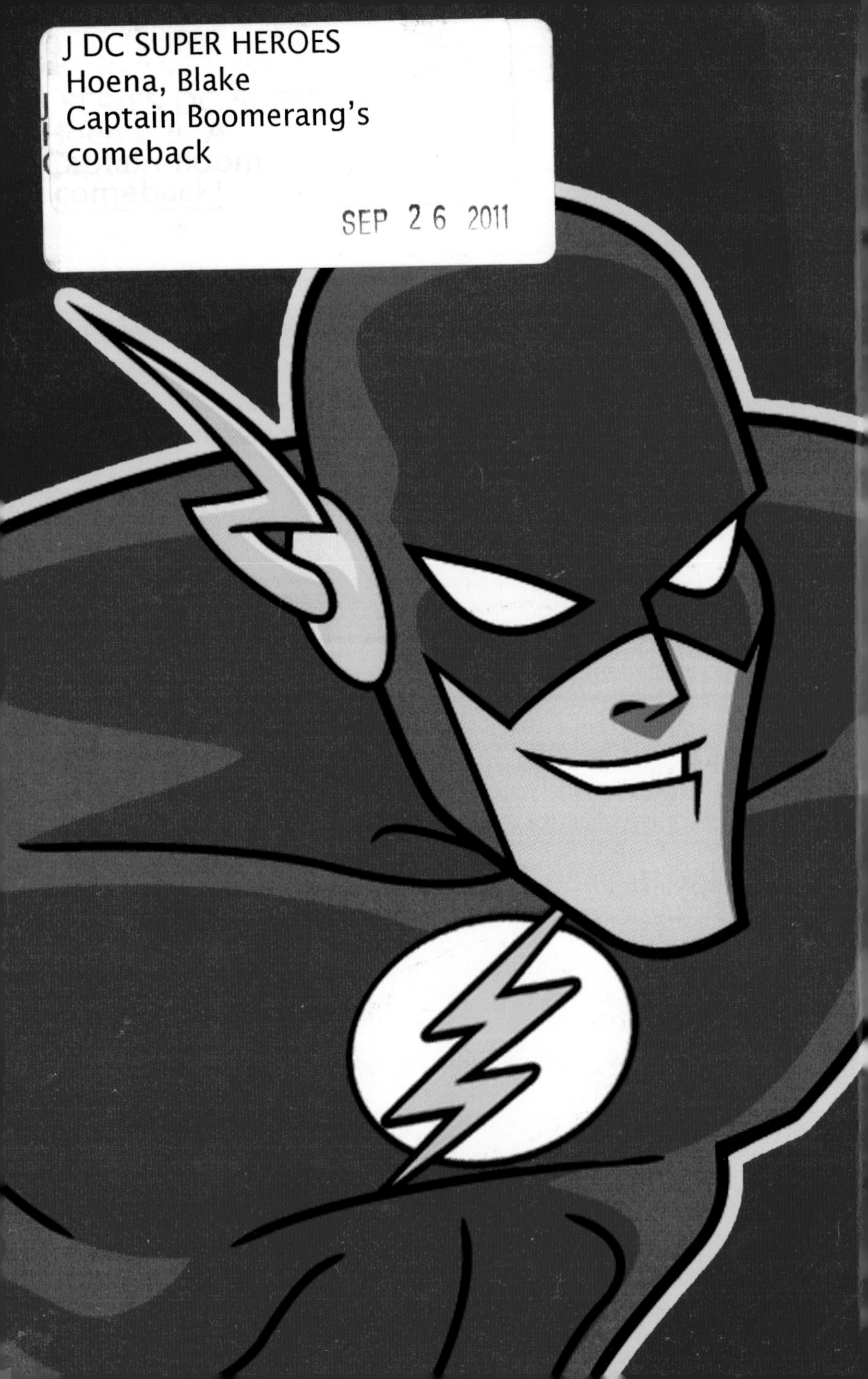